Alexandra

D1585074

*This book belongs to*

megan

Emily

Ben

# CONTENTS

# NODDY

## ANNUAL 2004

**Pedigree**®

Published by Pedigree Books Limited
Beech Hill House, Walnut Gardens, Exeter, Devon EX4 4DG.

E-mail books@pedigreegroup.co.uk

Published 2003

© and ™ Enid Blyton Limited (a Chorion Company). All rights reserved.

£7.50

# WELCOME TO TOYLAND

## HELLO, EVERYONE!

My name is Noddy and I live in a special part of Toyland called Toy Town. I have been very busy today, giving the Toy Town fire engine a good clean. Dinah Doll asked me to do it - she's our new Fire Chief, you see. You can read all about how she trained my friends and me to be good firefighters later in the annual. There are lots of other marvellous stories for you, too, as well as puzzles, rhymes and games. Before I give the fire engine a last polish, let me tell you about my Toyland friends...

# NODDY'S CAR

When I have finished cleaning the fire engine, I think I shall wash my little red and yellow taxi. Then it will be all ready to take passengers around Toy Town again. Everyone knows the "Parp! Parp!" of my car horn.

# BIG-EARS

Big-Ears the Brownie lives in Toadstool Wood and can often be seen riding his bicycle around Toy Town. He is my best friend and is especially helpful when I'm having trouble with those naughty goblins!

# DINAH DOLL

When Dinah Doll is not busy being Toy Town's Fire Chief, she runs my favourite stall in Toy Town market. If I need to buy a special present, I know that she will have just the right thing!

# TESSIE BEAR

Tessie Bear is another of my good friends. So is her bouncy dog, Bumpy - we have lots of fun together, but sometimes his bouncing gets me into trouble! Tessie Bear makes the best cakes ever and loves to share them with us all.

# MR. PLOD

Mr. Plod is Toy Town's policeman. Some of my friends are a little afraid of him because he is so stern, but we are all glad to see him when Sly and Gobbo have played one of their naughty tricks.

# MASTER TUBBY BEAR

Mr. and Mrs. Tubby Bear's son is Master Tubby Bear. He is another one of Toy Town's firefighters. Sometimes he can be very mischievous, as you'll soon find out.

# MARTHA MONKEY

My friend Martha Monkey is a firefighter, too. We also play on the same football team - you can read about what happened when we played against the Skittles team later in this annual.

# SLY

Wherever Gobbo goes, Sly goes too, which means double trouble. In the first story, you can read about how they tried to take all my customers in one of their naughtiest tricks ever!

# GOBBO

Of all the sneaky goblins that live in Toyland's Dark Wood, Gobbo is the naughtiest. He and his best friend, Sly, are always playing tricks on me and stealing my shopping!

# HERE'S NODDY

Here he comes along the street,
A nicer boy you will not meet,
He'll take you anywhere in his car,
He'll never tell you it's too far,
Give him a job that takes a while -
He'll do it happily, with a smile,
This nodding boy helps anybody,
What's his name? It's little Noddy!

# SHOPPING BASKETS

Noddy is always happy to do people's shopping for them. Today, Tessie Bear has asked him to buy some fruit, and Big-Ears would like the things needed to make cucumber sandwiches for afternoon tea.

Noddy has finished the shopping, but everything has got mixed up on the way back. Use a pencil to draw a line from each item and put it in the right basket: the pink spotty one for Tessie Bear's shopping and the red and yellow one for Big-Ears' shopping.

# NODDY AND THE NEW TAXI

It was a busy day in Toy Town, especially for Noddy and his little red and yellow taxi. He had already taken lots of passengers here and there before driving Dinah Doll to the train station. She was just in time to get on the Toyland Express.

Noddy said goodbye to Dinah Doll and set off for the High Street to pick up his next passenger, Mr. Wobbly Man. "There's Mr. Wobbly Man," said Noddy to his car, "but why is he talking to those naughty goblins, I wonder?"

Noddy was surprised to see Mr. Wobbly Man go with Sly and Gobbo. "Sorry, Noddy!" he called back, as they rode away. "Their first ride is free!" "Yes, you're not the only taxi in Toyland anymore!" cackled Gobbo.

Noddy was puzzled. "I suppose Toyland can have two taxis," he sighed. Big-Ears was cycling along and stopped to say hello. "I saw what happened," he said, "but you have been the only taxi for rather a long time."

Noddy decided Big-Ears was right. After all, there were always plenty of passengers to drive around. "We'll soon find another customer, little car," he said. "Oh, look! There's Mrs. Skittle needing a ride somewhere."

Before Noddy had chance to speak to Mrs. Skittle, the goblins sped in front of him and reached her first. "Free rides with us, Mrs. Skittle!" Gobbo called to her. Mrs. Skittle frowned: "I'd rather go with Noddy, thank you."

Mrs. Skittle got into Noddy's car. "Thank you for coming with me, Mrs. Skittle," Noddy smiled, as they drove away.

"Why did she go with him?" spluttered Sly. "Because everyone loves Noddy," Gobbo sneered. "We'll have to think of something."

The goblins did think of something. That night, they crept into Noddy's garage while Toy Town was sleeping. Whatever were they doing?

After breakfast the next morning, Noddy went to his garage. "Come on, little car," he said, opening the door. "Time for work."

Noddy set off as he usually did. When his car sped up a little, he tried to put the brake on. "Slow down, little car," he said, but the car went even faster. "Stop!" Noddy shouted, swerving so as not to bump into Martha Monkey.

Noddy's car let out an alarmed 'Parp! Parp!' as it hurtled on. "What's wrong?" shouted Noddy. "Stop, I said!" Noddy's car bumped into one thing after another until it finally crashed into a lamp post and came to a stop.

Mr. Plod was furious. "I'm arresting you for dangerous driving, Noddy," he frowned. "You and your car are coming to the police station."

Noddy's passengers had to use the goblins' taxi while he was in the police station. "Two coins, please," Sly said to Mrs. Skittle.

Mrs. Skittle was astonished. "But Noddy only charges one coin!" she protested. "Noddy's not here!" growled Sly. "Two coins!"

The naughty goblins took all Noddy's customers and charged them twice as much. How everyone missed Noddy and his little car!

Noddy told Mr. Plod and Big-Ears how his car had gone out of control. "Mr. Sparks can't find anything wrong with your car, Noddy," Mr. Plod said sternly. "If the problem isn't mechanical," said Big-Ears, "it must be magical."

"That's it! Sly and Gobbo must have put a Silly Spell on Noddy's car!" explained Big-Ears. Mr. Plod went to find the goblins and spotted them speeding in their taxi. "Stop in the name of Plod!" he boomed.

Sly and Gobbo admitted to putting the Silly Spell on Noddy's car. Mr. Plod made them take the spell back before marching them away. "Come on, little car," Noddy smiled. "It's time for us to find some passengers!" So they did!

# TAXI, PLEASE!

Noddy's little taxi is red and yellow. What sort of car would you like? Use your pencil to draw in your own special car. The wheels are already there to help you. When you're happy with it, colour it in however you like – you could even have a spotty car!

Noddy is always busy in his taxi. Here are some of the passengers he drives round Toy Town. Use your pencil to fill in the letters missing from their names.

Mr. J_m_o

D_n_h D_ll

T_s_ie B_a_

Mr. Sp_r_s

# RHYME WITH SLY

This naughty goblin is called Sly. Look at the things on this page and colour in the two that rhyme with 'Sly'. There are two more rhyming pairs. Colour them in as you say them, then use your pencil to match them up.

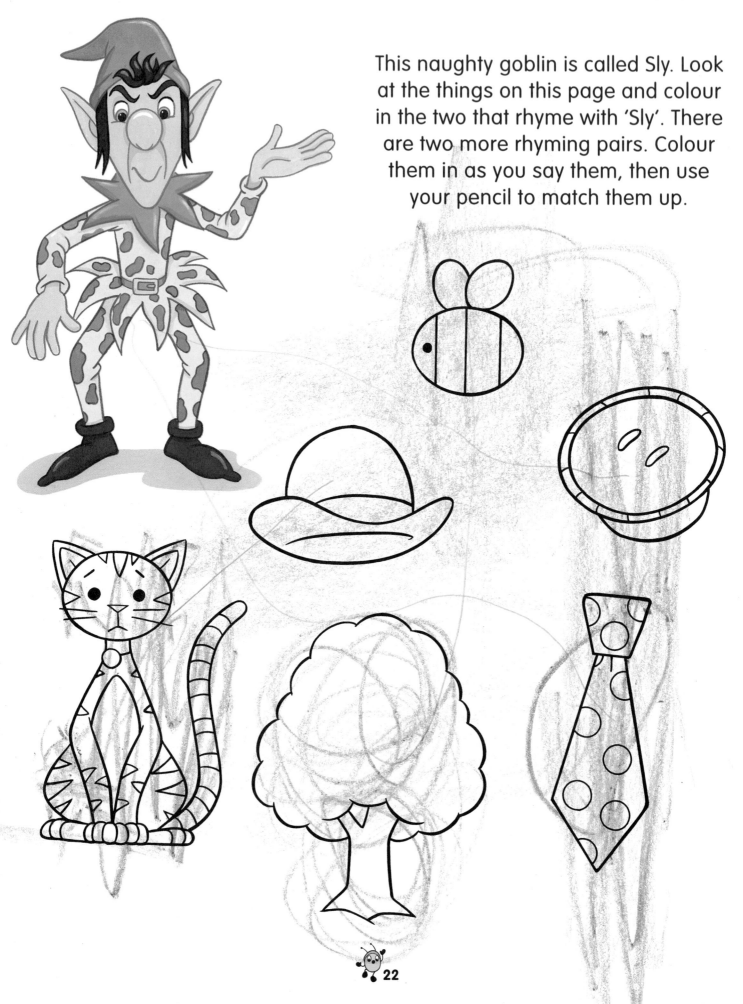

# CATCH THOSE GOBLINS

Those goblins from the Dark Wood
Are such a naughty pair,
They play tricks on poor Noddy
That no one else would dare!

They once took all his money
And hid up in a tree,
As they ran off with Noddy's bag,
Sly shouted, "Can't catch me!"

But Mr. Plod did catch them,
In the wood he found a clue,
He frowned and in his big, loud voice
Boomed, "Goblins! I know it's you!"

He took them back to Toy Town
And put them in his jail,
"I don't know why you bother," he said.
"You know I never fail!"

# TRAFFIC JAM

Sly and Gobbo have been following Noddy around to try
and steal his customers, but look what has happened. They were
so busy eating jam tarts that they weren't paying attention and
have crashed into Noddy. Silly old goblins!

Look at the two pictures and see if you can spot the
five differences between them. When you have found them all,
use your pens or crayons to colour the picture below, copying the
colours from the opposite page.

# NODDY AND THE MISSING CAKES

Noddy has made some lemon fairy cakes. He takes them out of the oven.

Here is Tessie Bear. "Mmm, they smell delicious, Noddy," she says.

"Leave them out to cool, Noddy," says Tessie. "Then we'll eat them later."

Noddy leaves the cakes to cool on the window sill and they go out.

Noddy takes Tessie Bear home. "See you later, Tessie," he calls to her.

Noddy comes home to find that his cakes have gone. "Oh, no!" he cries.

Noddy goes to the police station and tells Mr. Plod about the missing cakes.

Mr. Plod says, "Perhaps the cakes were so light, the breeze blew them away."

Noddy and Mr. Plod go to Noddy's House-For-One to look for clues.

"This is the exact spot where my cakes went missing, Mr. Plod," says Noddy.

Mr. Plod looks. "Hmm, I see," he says, sternly. Bumpy Dog comes to help.

"A-ha!" says Mr. Plod. "I knew I would find a clue sooner or later, Noddy!"

"I used those gloves to take the cakes out of the oven," Noddy explains.

Noddy goes outside and finds some cake crumbs. He shouts for Mr. Plod.

Noddy and Mr. Plod go for a drive to see if they can find any more clues.

"Stop the car at once!" shouts Mr. Plod, suddenly. "I see a cake being eaten!"

Mr. Sparks bought his cake. "My cakes didn't have raisins in," Noddy sighs.

Mr. Plod sees Big-Ears carrying cakes on his bicycle. "Stop!" he shouts.

Big-Ears explains that they are orange cakes. Mr. Plod tastes one to be sure.

"Anything that is missing usually turns up in the Dark Wood," says Big-Ears.

Big-Ears is right. "I've eaten too much!" groans Sly. "Me, too!" moans Gobbo.

Mr. Plod finds the goblins. "Eaten too many cakes, have we?" he booms.

"We solved the case," says Noddy, "but I still don't have my cakes."

Someone arrives with a fresh batch of lemon cakes. Well done, Tessie Bear!

# NODDY'S YUMMY TREATS

Noddy loves baking. He was very upset when his lemon cakes went missing, wasn't he? Do you like to help make cakes and biscuits? What are your favourites? On these pages are some of Noddy's favourites. Look at each row and say what teatime treats you can see. Then count them and use your pencil to write the number in the box.

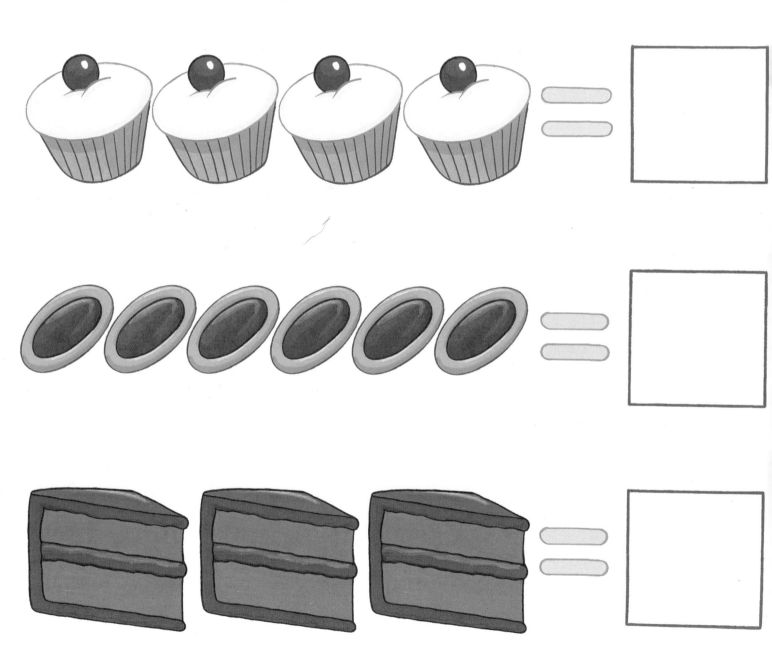

# THE ICING ON THE CAKE

Tessie Bear loves baking, too. Look at the lovely cake she has made! You can decorate it for her. Use your pens or crayons to make the cake as colourful and yummy-looking as you can.

# I LOVE TO BAKE!

I'm in the kitchen, baking cakes,
I stir the mix till my arm aches!

I love fruit pies and treacle tart,
I'm caked in flour before I start!

I love to make up snow white icing
To spread on a big cake for slicing.

I love the smell of hot bread rolls,
I love to use up lots of bowls.

I love to mix, I love to bake -
The best bit is the mess I make!

# PARKING TICKET

Mr. Plod is very cross. Someone has parked
a great big something in the middle of Toy Town,
blocking the street. Join to dots to find out what it is,
then say who you think may have left it there.

# MR. PLOD IS STERN

High above your head he looms
And in a big, loud voice he booms:
"Stop in the name of Plod, I say!"
So sternly you'll want to run away,
But he's just checking you're all right,
Not meaning to give you a fright,
If you're in Toy Town you'll soon learn
That Mr. Plod is usually stern,
A policeman has to be that way
To keep law and order, come what may,
But give him cake and in a while,
You'll soon see this policeman smile!

# THE CHRISTMAS FLOWERS

It was two days before Christmas and Noddy was finishing his shopping in Toy Town market. He wanted to buy some special flowers for Tessie Bear. Flowers were Tessie Bear's favourite thing. He went to Dinah Doll's stall to look for some.

"Hello, Dinah Doll," said Noddy. "Do you have any special Christmas flowers on your stall?" Dinah Doll told Noddy that he was just in time. "All I have left are these five lovely red ones," she added. "Do you like them?"

Noddy said he loved the flowers and bought all five of them. "Tessie Bear will be so pleased when I give her these," he said to himself. He drove home with his shopping, whistling his favourite Christmas songs as he went.

When Noddy arrived at his House-For-One, he took his parcels in first. "I shall come back for the flowers in a moment, little car," he said.

Noddy came back to get his flowers from the car. "One, two, three, four... FOUR?" he said, puzzled. "That's funny. I'm sure I bought five."

Noddy looked at his shopping. "It's all there except the missing flower," he frowned. "Tessie Bear and Big-Ears are coming tomorrow evening and I want everything to be right. Maybe Dinah Doll still has it."

Back at the market, Dinah Doll said she was certain Noddy had left with five flowers. As he was leaving, he saw Tessie Bear - with one of the flowers! "Hello, Noddy!" she called. "I'm looking forward to tomorrow!"

Noddy was disappointed. "Someone has given Tessie a flower just like the ones I bought her," he said to himself. "Oh!" he gasped, when he got home. "Now there are only one, two, three flowers. What's going on?"

Noddy remembered he still had to get mince pies for Christmas Eve with his friends. Bumpy Dog bounded in at just the right moment.

Noddy sternly told Bumpy Dog to watch over the special flowers while he popped to the baker's shop for his mince pies.

When Noddy got back to his House-For-One, Bumpy Dog was nowhere to be seen. "Where is Bumpy Dog?" he wondered. "Oh, no!" he exclaimed. "Now I only have one, two flowers left. This is very peculiar."

Noddy went to look for Bumpy Dog. While he was out, he saw Mr. Plod and stopped to tell him about his disappearing flowers. "Disappearing flowers?" Mr. Plod chuckled. "Maybe you've forgotten how to count, Noddy!"

Noddy went to see if Bumpy Dog had gone home. Stepping inside Tessie Bear's house, he stopped and stared - she had three red flowers now. "Aren't they lovely?" she said, thinking Noddy liked looking at them.

Noddy was so fed up he went home to bed. When he got up the next morning, there was only one flower left. "I don't know," he sighed.

Noddy had been so busy puzzling over the missing flowers that he had left his car out all night in the snow. "I'm sorry, little car," he said.

Mr. Plod was passing. Noddy was just telling him about the other flower, when Mr. Plod blew his whistle. "There's your culprit, Noddy!" he boomed. "Bumpy Dog, stop in the name of Plod! That's Noddy's flower!"

They chased Bumpy Dog home and saw him give Tessie Bear the flower. "That's your thief," said Mr. Plod. Noddy had to laugh. "He's more of a delivery dog, really," he chuckled. "Thank you, Noddy," Tessie Bear smiled.

That evening, Tessie Bear and Big-Ears came to Noddy's house for tea and to give each other their presents. "Where's your other present for Tessie Bear, Noddy?" Big-Ears asked. "Ah," smiled Noddy, "it's a long story..."

# GOING, GOING, GONE!

Noddy had five flowers
When he went through his door,
He came back out to get them
And then there were four!

He went to Toy Town market
To go back and see
If Dinah Doll still had it,
But then there were three!

Noddy did feel puzzled,
What should he do?
He went off to the baker's,
He came back - there were two!

Fed-up Noddy went to bed
When the day was done,
He woke up the next morning
To find there was just one!

While Noddy talked to Mr. Plod,
Bumpy Dog did run,
He had the flower in his mouth,
Poor Noddy - he had none!

# SNOW PRINTS

Have you ever looked at tracks in the snow? People and animals leave all sorts of funny prints when they walk! Next time it snows, see how many different tracks you can find, then make some of your own. Look at the tracks below and match them to the person or animal you think made them.

# OH, CHRISTMAS TREE

Noddy is going to decorate his Christmas tree and you can help him if you like. Cut out this page first, then cut out the decorations and stick them on the tree with paper glue to make it look beautiful. Make sure you have finished doing the puzzle on the back of this page before you start!

49

# SO MANY STORIES

Look at all my bedtime stories,
Must I choose just one?
Why not read me two or three?
I think that would be fun!

All right then, I'll hear only one
And put the rest away,
But you must promise me you'll read
Them all another day!

# NODDY'S BEDTIME STORIES

## What Strange Weather!
## Bumpy Dog's Visit

# WHAT STRANGE WEATHER!

It was a very windy day in Toy Town, but the sun was shining brightly. In fact, it was a perfect kite-flying day. Noddy searched for his kite and put it in his car. He was looking forward to playing with it, but first he had to pick up some milk from the dairy and deliver it to Tessie Bear.

When Bumpy Dog heard the 'Parp! Parp!' of Noddy's car, he bounded out to greet him. He was so excited to see Noddy when he got out of his car that he jumped over the gate and knocked him down like a skittle.

"Goodness me, that wind is strong today," chuckled Noddy. "It blew me right over. Was it the wind, or was it you, Bumpy Dog?"

Noddy lifted the huge milk can out of the car and was struggling up the path with it when Tessie Bear opened the door.

"Hello, Noddy. Thank you for bringing my milk," she smiled. "Just leave it there for now. Oh, you've brought your kite! It's certainly windy enough for kites today!"

"Yes, I'm on my way to find somewhere to fly it," said Noddy.

Tessie Bear told Noddy that if he promised to deliver some of her hen's eggs to Dinah Doll, he could fly his kite in her garden. Noddy was pleased. Tessie Bear gave him the eggs and went inside to make some cakes. Noddy put the eggs down on the milk can and went to get his kite from the car.

"Come on, then, Bumpy," said Noddy, opening the gate to the garden. "Arf! Arf!" barked Bumpy Dog excitedly. Noddy had been flying his kite for only a minute or so, before he heard clucking.

"Oh, no!" he cried. "I left the gate open and the hens have escaped!"

Noddy ran out to get the hens back. Looking for somewhere to put his kite, he tied it to the heavy milk can.

"Come back, hens!" he shouted, running down the road after them with a jingle-jing of his hat. It was so windy, do you know what happened? The kite was carried way up into the sky, taking the milk and eggs with it. By the time Noddy brought the hens back, his kite was out of reach and heading for Toy Town.

"Follow that kite!" he shouted. Dinah Doll was serving Mr. Sparks at her market stall. She was still saying, "What lovely weather it is today," when it began to rain.

"Oh!" she exclaimed, surprised. "Would you like to buy an umbrella too, Mr. Sparks?"

Nearby, Miss Pink Cat was chatting to Big-Ears when she also felt the rain. A big drop fell on her paw and she peered at it.

"White rain?" she said, astonished. Licking it, she added, "It's milk!"

"Nonsense!" Big-Ears laughed. "I've seen all sorts of weather, but I've never seen it rain milk."

"I know milk when I taste it, Big-Ears," Miss Pink Cat insisted, "I've been drinking it all my life!"

Big-Ears was about to reply, when SPLAT! An egg dropped right in the middle of Mr. Plod's helmet. Then SPLAT! A second one fell on his shoulder. He was furious.

"Clockwork Mouse!" he boomed to the nearest toy. "Stop in the name of Plod! Did you throw these eggs at me?"

"No, Mr. Plod!" replied Clockwork Mouse. "I don't have any eggs on me!" SPLAT! An egg landed on his head.

"You do now!" Big-Ears chuckled. Master Tubby Bear had just finished his milk shake. "I wish I had some more," he said. PLIP! PLOP! Milk dripped into his glass from above. "I wish I had a new bike," he added, looking up hopefully.

Mr. Plod looked up with a puzzled frown.

"This is a very strange weather day," he said. He stood in the busy market and shouted, "Attention, everyone! There is a reward for anyone who can solve 'The Case Of The Strange Weather'."

Noddy ran up, out of breath.

"I'm so sorry, everyone," he said, "it's my fault...and the wind's. It blew away my kite, and my kite was tied to Tessie Bear's milk and Dinah Doll's eggs, and - and -"

Big-Ears let out a roar of laughter.

"Why are you laughing, Big-Ears?" Mr. Plod asked sternly.

"Because you have to give a reward to the little rascal who started all this!" explained Big-Ears.

"Oh!" said Mr. Plod. Then he began to laugh heartily, too.

"Aren't you cross with me, Mr. Plod?" Noddy asked.

"No, Noddy," smiled Mr. Plod. "This is one the funniest things that has happened in Toy Town. "

Noddy was glad that he was not in trouble, but he did not want his reward. He was too worried about what he was going to say to Tessie Bear about her missing milk and eggs.

"Why don't I just give you enough to pay for Tessie Bear's things?" Mr. Plod suggested. "Then everyone is happy."

"What a good idea," said Noddy. "Thank you, Mr. Plod."

"No, thank you, Noddy," Mr. Plod replied, "for giving us all such a good laugh today!"

# BUMPY DOG'S VISIT

Noddy often went to see Tessie Bear for tea and cakes. One afternoon, she mentioned to him that there was a day trip she would like to go on.

"It's a shame I'll miss it," she said. "You see, I can't take Bumpy Dog with me, and I can't leave him by himself."

"I will look after Bumpy Dog for you," Noddy offered.

"Noddy, are you sure?" Tessie Bear asked, surprised. "Bumpy Dog can be quite naughty sometimes."

"Of course I'm sure," said Noddy. "I'll be the best dog-sitter in the world!"

On the day of Tessie Bear's trip, Noddy went to her house early to take her to the train station.

"Goodbye, Tessie Bear," he called, waving. "Have a good trip!" Noddy decided to take Bumpy Dog back to his House-For-One for breakfast. Bumpy Dog was very good in the car to begin with, sitting in the front like any other passenger.

"I knew this would be easy," said Noddy, but Bumpy Dog soon started to fidget. Then he sprang on to the back seat and jumped from side to side, barking excitedly.

"Bumpy Dog, come back into the front!" Noddy shouted. Bumpy did as he was told, but tried to get into Noddy's lap and lick his face.

"No, Bumpy!" Noddy cried. "I can't see where I'm - oof!" BUMP! The car went off the road. Noddy told Bumpy Dog that he really had to keep still, otherwise they would never get home.

When they at last reached Noddy's House-For-One, Noddy took Bumpy inside and told him to be good while he got the food from the car. When Noddy returned he could hardly believe his eyes.

"Bumpy Dog!" he exclaimed. "What a mess you've made already! Have breakfast outside and keep out of the way until I've cleaned up."

Noddy tidied up, then went out to see if Bumpy Dog would like to go for a walk. He could not find him anywhere.

"Oh, no!" wailed Noddy. "Bumpy Dog has
run away! I shall have to find him."
Noddy looked first in the market. He asked Dinah
Doll if she had seen Bumpy Dog.
"I have, Noddy," she
replied, crossly,
"he's broken one
of my best
teacups."
Noddy said he
was very sorry
and paid for the cup.
He went on to Miss Pink Cat's
ice-cream parlour and BUMP! He
slipped on some ice-cream.
"Ouch!" said Noddy.
"That naughty Bumpy Dog made this mess!"
Miss Pink Cat told him. "He's knocked cornets all over my floor, too."
Noddy explained that he was looking after Bumpy Dog
and helped Miss Pink Cat clean up.

Noddy tried Mr. Sparks' garage next.
"Have you seen Bumpy Dog, Mr. Sparks?" called Noddy. "Yes!
Look," Mr. Sparks replied, pointing to some oily pawprints on
his forecourt. "He knocked an oildrum over and paddled
through the oil. What a mess!"
Again, Noddy had to say sorry and
give Mr. Sparks some money for
his trouble. He knew he would
have to tell Mr. Plod that Bumpy
was on the loose.
"Bumpy Dog's in jail, Noddy"
Mr. Plod said, sternly.
"In jail?" Noddy cried. "But I'm
supposed to be looking after
him and if he's in jail, what
will I tell Tessie Bear?
Oh, my goodness, oh -"

"Calm down," Mr. Plod smiled. "I only put him in there until someone collected him. I'll let him out."

"Thank you, Mr. Plod," said Noddy, relieved. He hugged Bumpy Dog and decided it might be best if he took him back to Tessie Bear's house.

When Tessie returned at teatime, the house was very quiet.

"Noddy?" she called softly. There, on the settee, were Noddy and Bumpy Dog, sleeping soundly.

"How lovely," Tessie Bear smiled. "Noddy has been the best pet-sitter, after all!"

# DREAMS, PLEASE

Now it's time to go to sleep,
I hope I have a dream!
I might dream of a football game
- I'll score for the winning team!

Maybe I will dream I'm flying
Bird-like, through the clouds,
Or on a super magic carpet,
Swooping past the crowds.

Perhaps I'll sail a pirate ship,
Or roll in snow so white,
What's that? I need to sleep to dream?
Oh, yes - of course! Goodnight!

# OH, BUMPY DOG!

In the story, Bumpy Dog was quite a handful for poor Noddy! Count all the things he knocked over or made a mess with and use a pencil to practice writing your numbers while you do so.

1 1 1 1 1

2 2 2 2 2

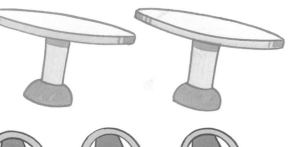

3 3 3 3 3

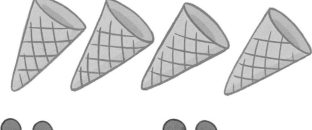

4 4 4 4

5 5 5

# WHICH WEATHER?

Noddy and his friends saw it raining milk and eggs, didn't they?
What is rain usually made of? How many other sorts of weather can you think of?
Look at the things below and say in what sort of weather you would use each one.

We see a rainbow when it is sunny and rainy at the same time.
Use your pens or crayons to colour this picture of Noddy
having splishy splashy fun near a rainbow.

# HAPPY BIRTHDAY, NODDY!

Join in this story by saying what the pictures are as they appear.

Little  usually has to work on his birthday.

One year, he had to deliver a  to . As he

was putting it in his car,  ran up and knocked

right over. CRASH! went the . "Oh, no!" said

. "That  is for  and whatever is in it has

broken." He opened the . In it was a lovely

teapot.  rushed to the market and bought

another one from Dinah Doll. At last, he delivered

the . "You keep it," smiled . "It's your

birthday present. Happy birthday, !"

# BUMPY DOG'S BALL GAMES

As Noddy wandered
through the park,
He heard the sound of
Bumpy Dog's bark,
"What's that you've found?
A ball, you say?
And you're asking me to
come and play?"

So Noddy said he would
play ball,
He held it up and let it fall,
Then threw it hard,
so Bumpy ran,
"Go, Bumpy Dog, as fast
as you can!"

Bumpy stopped it with his paws,
Then brought it back,
held in his jaws,
But then a POP! The ball was gone,
"Oh, Bumpy Dog. What have
you done?"

Bumpy Dog let out a whine,
As if to say "That ball was mine!"
So Noddy went to Dinah's stall
And bought his friend a brand
new ball.

# THE GREAT TRAIN CHASE

It was market day in Toy Town. Dinah Doll had the best stall in the market, selling all sorts of delightful things. She was so busy setting up her stall that she did not see Master Tubby Bear giving her a helping hand.

Master Tubby Bear arranged the flowers a little too eagerly. CRASH! The flower bucket tipped over, emptying water and flowers all over the floor. "Master Tubby Bear!" cried Dinah Doll. "Please be more careful!"

Dinah Doll began to clear up the mess. "I was only trying to help," Master Tubby Bear told her. "I'd like to run a stall like you. Would you show me how?" "Not now," Dinah replied. "Perhaps I will when you're a little older."

Master Tubby Bear came across Noddy's car. "I would love to drive around like Noddy," he said, climbing into the driver's seat.

"Master Tubby Bear!" Noddy exclaimed when he saw him. "You're not old enough to drive. Move over and you can come for a ride."

Noddy had to go and pick up Mr. Jumbo from the train station. "But I want to be a taxi driver," Master Tubby Bear told him. "Won't you show me how to drive?" "Perhaps I will when you're a little older," Noddy chuckled.

Noddy and Master Tubby Bear went to the platform and watched the Toyland Express coming in. "I love trains!" Tubby Bear exclaimed.

While Noddy went to find Mr. Jumbo, Master Tubby Bear went to ask if he could drive the train. "You're too young!" laughed the driver.

The driver went to get a cup of tea. Master Tubby Bear was fed up of being told he was too young to do things. He climbed up into the train and pressed some buttons until it moved forward. "Stop!" Noddy cried.

Chuffity-chuff, chuffity-chuff went the Toyland Express. "This is easy," chuckled Master Tubby Bear. "I'm being a proper train driver!"

Noddy ran into the police station. "Mr. Plod! Come quickly!" he cried. "Master Tubby Bear has driven away in the Toyland Express!"

The Toyland Express went faster and faster. "Where are the brakes?" Master Tubby Bear murmured, pressing more buttons. Then he began to panic. "Oh, dear!" he wailed. "Slow down, train! You're going too quickly!"

Master Tubby Bear could not make the train slow down. It went so fast that suddenly, it came off the rails and sped into a field. "Oh, my goodness!" cried Master Tubby Bear. "What's going on?" shouted the passengers.

Master Tubby Bear thought he should turn the train round. Perhaps if he could get it back to Toy Town, the driver could tell him how to stop it. Goodness, what a mess he made of the field! The farmer would be very cross indeed.

Master Tubby Bear steered the train into Toy Town, but still he could not stop it. CRASH! The train knocked over Miss Pink Cat's delivery of milk. "OH!" cried Miss Pink Cat, dropping all her ice-cream cones.

The train hurtled into Toy Town market. BUMP! It sent a cart of oranges flying. "Stop that train at once!" Mr. Plod shouted and blew his whistle. "I wish I could!" Master Tubby Bear replied. "I need some help! Stop, train!"

The train driver ran as fast as he could to catch up with the Toyland Express. He leaped into the driver's carriage and took the controls. The passengers were relieved and clapped with delight as the train began to slow down.

At last the train stopped and Master Tubby Bear jumped off. "Well, Master Tubby Bear?" boomed Mr. Plod. "I'm sorry, everyone," said the shame-faced bear. "Now I know that I'm NOT old enough to do everything!"

# TOYLAND TRAIN TIMES

The train driver has his train back now and everything is back to normal after Master Tubby Bear's train adventure. The Toyland Express is even running on time!

The Toyland Express leaves Toy Town at 3 o'clock.

What time does the Toyland Express arrive at the Village Of Bouncing Balls?

Noddy has to take some passengers to Toy Town station today. Use your pencil to draw in the train times that he needs to know.

Miss Pink Cat would like to catch the early train from Toy Town at 7 o'clock.

Mr. Wobbly man is going to catch the late morning train at 11 o'clock.

Martha Monkey wants to get an afternoon train at 2 o'clock.

Big-Ears is getting the teatime train at 5 o'clock.

# STOP THE TRAIN!

"I shall be the driver,"
Said Master Tubby Bear,
He climbed into the Toyland train
And what did he find there?
Levers, dials and buttons,
"What does this one do?
Now we're going down the track,
This is fun! Whoo! Whoo!

I'd like the train to stop now,
I'm ready for my tea,
Oh, no! It's going faster!
I've no idea, you see,
The others said I'm much too young,
I wish I'd understood,
Please help me stop this speeding train
Then I promise I'll be good!"

# 'T' IS FOR TRAIN

'T' is for train and Tubby Bear. Here are some of the things Master Tubby Bear saw on his train adventure. Colour in the ones that begin with the letter 't'. Can you think of any other words beginning with 't'? There is one thing on this page that does not begin with 't'. What letter does it begin with?

# HELLO, MASTER TUBBY BEAR

Master Tubby Bear has forgotten all about his train scare now that he has one of his favourite ice-creams to eat.

Use your crayons or felt-tip pens to colour in this picture of Master Tubby Bear. See if you can match the colours to those on the opposite page.

# TOY TOWN'S WINNING TEAM

Noddy is on his way to play football. He stops to talk to Mr. Wobbly Man.

"I love football, Noddy," says Mr. Wobbly Man. "I wish I could play, too."

"You can play on my team," Noddy smiles. "We're playing the Skittles."

Mr. Wobbly Man is delighted that Noddy invited him to play.

At the football ground, everyone is doing their warm-up exercises.

Mr. Wobbly Man tries to kick the ball too, but all he can do is wobble.

Martha Monkey is cross. "Why is he on our team?" she asks Noddy.

Mr. Wobbly Man heard her. "You're better off without me," he sighs.

"I'm sorry," says Noddy. "Why don't you watch and cheer us on?"

Here are the Skittles. "They look like a good team," says Noddy.

The whistle sounds and the match begins. The Skittles take the ball!

The Skittles score quickly. "It's a go-o-oal!" shout their Skittle supporters.

The Skittles are playing well. They even get the ball past Mr. Sparks.

Poor Martha tries her best, but she cannot stop another winning goal.

The match goes on and the Skittles get the ball again. Someone stop them!

The ball goes off, but Mr. Wobbly Man stops it getting lost in the bushes.

As Noddy walks over, his bell jingles, which means he has a good idea.

Now Martha Monkey is playing on the field. Who could the goalkeeper be?

It's Mr. Wobbly Man! None of the Skittles can get the ball past this goalie!

Noddy gets the ball after Mr. Wobbly Man's save - and he scores!

The Skittles try and try, but they cannot score again for the rest of the match.

Noddy scores another goal. What a player he is!

The final whistle means the game has finished. It's a draw!

Mr. Wobbly Man saved the match. Well done, Mr. Wobbly Man!

# FOOTBALL PRACTICE

Noddy and his friends are warming up for their football match.
Can you find eight footballs in the picture? When you have found them all, use your crayons or pens to colour the picture.

93

# GET READY TO GO

Noddy has packed his sports bag and is all ready to go and play football. Colour in the things below that you think you might need to play football. Which thing would you not need for a football match? Which game do you think you would need it for?

# A WOBBLY GOALIE

He's large and he's round
And he wears a pink top hat,
All he does is wobble
This way and that.

Football player Noddy said,
"Come and join in!"
He thought that this new player
Could help his team to win.

A great save! And another!
He's surely passed the test,
As far as goalies go,
Mr. Wobbly Man's the best!

# WHICH WAY TO THE MATCH?

Noddy is taking Mr. Wobbly Man to the next football match.
They feel sure they are going to win! Use a pencil or your finger to
show them which way to go.

# FIRE CHIEF DINAH

It was a very important day in Toy Town. Mr. Plod had called everyone to a special meeting in the town square. They all wondered why he had brought the fire engine with him.

"Good afternoon, everyone," he began. "As you all know, this is our fire engine. It has a hose, a blue light and a ladder."

"Does he think we haven't seen it before?" Master Tubby Bear whispered to Big-Ears.

"Ssh, listen," he replied.

"What it does not have, though," Mr. Plod carried on, "is a fire brigade. All our firefighters have gone to work in other Toyland towns."

Big-Ears nodded to Master Tubby Bear in a 'There you are' sort of way.

"So, first of all, I need someone to be in charge," Mr. Plod looked around the crowd. "A Fire Chief to lead the firefighters."

"What about Mr. Sparks?" suggested Noddy.

"I'm already busy driving the fire engine," Mr. Sparks explained. "Perhaps Dinah Doll would like to do it. She's very clever."

"Oh, yes!" everyone agreed together. "Dinah Doll for Fire Chief!"

Dinah Doll was proud to be Toy Town's Chief Firefighter and chose Noddy, Master Tubby Bear, Martha Monkey and Clockwork Mouse to be her helpers. She decided that the new fire brigade should have a practice the very next day.

"Today, we are going to pretend that the clock tower is on fire," she told her team. "This will be the fire alarm," she went on, holding up a large bell. "Ready? Go!"
DING-A-LING-A-LING-A-LING!
Dinah rang the bell as loudly as she could. Everyone panicked and ran this

way and

that,

bumping

into each other.

"Oh, dear," sighed Dinah Doll. Noddy ran to the ladder and pulled it out. It was much heavier than he thought it would be and it swung round, almost knocking Dinah Doll over. "Careful, Noddy!" she exclaimed.

Martha Monkey went to unravel the hose. "The hose is my job!" cried Master Tubby Bear, tugging at it. "No, it isn't!" Martha protested, snatching it back. Mr. Sparks turned the hose on, but still Martha and Master Tubby fought over it. SPLOOSH! The water shot out and squirted in all directions.

"Do stop it!" exclaimed Dinah Doll.

"You're soaking us!" Noddy protested.

"That's enough!" Dinah cried.

Dinah Doll made everyone sit down quietly and listen carefully.

"It's very important that we all work together, as a team," she explained. "First of all, you must learn to get to the fire engine quickly, without bumping into each other. Secondly, Martha and Master Tubby, the hose needs two people; when it's full of water it's too difficult for one person to hold. Finally, Noddy, the ladder is too heavy for you to manage by yourself, so Clockwork Mouse, you must help him. Now, let's try again."

The firefighters agreed that Dinah
was right. When she rang the bell, they ran
in a line to the fire engine. Martha Monkey and
Master Tubby Bear worked together to aim the hose at
the pretend fire. Clockwork Mouse agreed to help Noddy
with the heavy ladder. He held it against the wall so that it was
safe for Noddy to go up.
"That's more like it!" Dinah smiled. "Now we look like real firefighters.
Well done, team!"

The next day, there was a real emergency at Tessie Bear's house. Dinah Doll rang the bell and everyone ran to the fire engine. They did it quickly and sensibly because they had practiced.

"Ready, Mr. Sparks!" Dinah called out. "We need to get to Tessie Bear's house!" The fire engine sped through Toy Town with its siren on and its blue light flashing. They soon reached the house on fire.

"Oh, thank you for coming so quickly!" Tessie Bear exclaimed. "Please help my poor Bumpy Dog! He was so frightened of the fire that he jumped up on to the roof and can't get down!"

While Martha Monkey and Master Tubby Bear worked the hose to put out the fire downstairs, Clockwork Mouse held the ladder steady for Noddy to climb up to the roof.

"Hello, Bumpy Dog," Noddy said, holding his arms out. "It's all right now, come down with me." Bumpy Dog was very pleased to see Noddy and eagerly jumped to him.

Noddy carried Bumpy Dog down the ladder and took him to Tessie Bear. Bumpy Dog was safe, the fire was out and everyone agreed that the new fire brigade had done a very good job indeed.

"You saved my dear Bumpy Dog," smiled Tessie Bear, hugging her dog. "Thank you all."

Dinah Doll was delighted with her team and gathered them together to thank them.
"We all worked together and remembered what we had practiced," she said.
"Now we are ready for any emergency. Well done!"
"We did do a good job," Noddy agreed, "but it was all thanks to you, Dinah."
"Yes, Noddy's right," nodded Martha Monkey. "Come on, everyone - three cheers
for the best Fire Chief ever! Hip, hip, hooray! Hip, hip, hooray! Hip, hip, hooray!"

# EMERGENCY!

Nee-naw! Nee-naw!
What's that noise?
Nee-naw! Nee-naw!
It's the firefighting toys!

Splish, splash! Splish, splash!
They've turned their hoses on,
Splish, splash! Splish, splash!
Soon the flames have gone.

Hip, hip, hooray!
The panic's over now,
Hip, hip, hooray!
Chief Dinah, take a bow!

# FIRE ENGINE FUN

All these fire engines look the same, but only one is the fire engine that Mr. Sparks drives. The others each have something missing. Point to the one you think is the Toy Town fire engine, and say what is missing from the other three.

# REACH THE FIRE FIRST

Mr. Straw's barn is on fire, but only Noddy and Dinah Doll are able to go and put it out. You and a friend can help them if you can find a dice and two counters.

One of the cows is in the road. Miss a turn while you go round it.

Take a counter for each player and put them on the start. Take turns to throw the dice and work your way round Toyland, making sure you throw a six to start. You could make fire engine noises as you go! On the way are special ladybirds: if you land on a ladybird, you can go on two spaces. Watch out for goblins, though! The first one to reach the barn to put out the fire is the winner.